MISSING!

Flame

Have you seen this kitten?

Flame is a magic kitten of royal blood, missing from his own world.
His uncle, Ebony, is very keen that he is found quickly.
Flame may be hard to spot as he often appears in a
variety of fluffy kitten colours but you can recognize him
by his big emerald eyes and whiskers that crackle with magic!

He is believed to be looking for a young friend to take care of him.

Could it be you?

If you find this very special kitten please let Ebony,
ruler of the Lion Throne, know.

Sue Bentley's books for children often include animals or fairies. She lives in Northampton and enjoys reading, going to the cinema, and sitting watching the frogs and newts in her garden pond. If she hadn't been a writer she would probably have been a skydiver or brain surgeon. The main reason she writes is that she can drink pots and pots of tea while she's typing. She has met and owned many cats and each one has brought a special sort of magic to her life.

Magic Kitten

Sparkling Steps

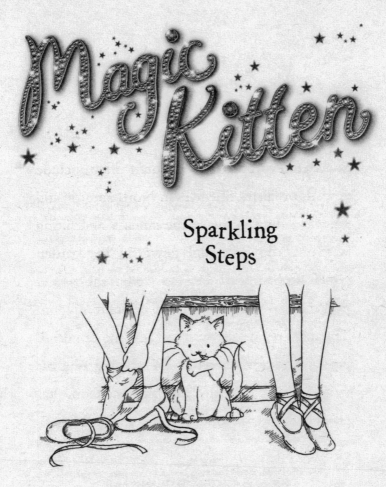

SUE BENTLEY

Illustrated by Angela Swan

PUFFIN

Biba — our chatty tortie-tabby girl

PUFFIN BOOKS

Published by the Penguin Group
Penguin Books Ltd, 80 Strand, London WC2R ORL, England
Penguin Group (USA) Inc., 375 Hudson Street, New York, New York 10014, USA
Penguin Group (Canada), 90 Eglinton Avenue East, Suite 700, Toronto, Ontario, Canada M4P 2Y3
(a division of Pearson Penguin Canada Inc.)
Penguin Ireland, 25 St Stephen's Green, Dublin 2, Ireland (a division of Penguin Books Ltd)
Penguin Group (Australia), 250 Camberwell Road, Camberwell, Victoria 3124, Australia
(a division of Pearson Australia Group Pty Ltd)
Penguin Books India Pvt Ltd, 11 Community Centre, Panchsheel Park, New Delhi – 110 017, India
Penguin Group (NZ), 67 Apollo Drive, Mairangi Bay, Auckland 1310, New Zealand
(a division of Pearson New Zealand Ltd)
Penguin Books (South Africa) (Pty) Ltd, 24 Sturdee Avenue, Rosebank, Johannesburg 2196, South Africa

Penguin Books Ltd, Registered Offices: 80 Strand, London WC2R ORL, England

penguin.com

Published 2007
2

Text copyright © Sue Bentley, 2007
Illustrations copyright © Angela Swan, 2007
All rights reserved

The moral right of the author and illustrator has been asserted

Set in Bembo
Typeset by Palimpsest Book Production Limited, Grangemouth, Stirlingshire
Made and printed in England by Clays Ltd, St Ives plc

British Library Cataloguing in Publication Data
A CIP catalogue record for this book is available from the British Library

ISBN: 978-0-141-32155-4

Prologue

A terrifying growl sounded close by
and the young white lion froze. He had
hoped it was safe to return this time.
But he was wrong. He must act quickly.

Sparks ignited in Flame's fur and
there was a flash of bright white light.
Where he had stood now crouched a
tiny kitten with a round face and
velvety blue-grey fur.

An old grey lion limped forward from the shadows at the back of the cave. 'Prince Flame! You shouldn't be here. You must hide!'

'There is no time, Cirrus. Uncle Ebony is coming!' the little kitten mewed, trembling.

Cirrus reached out a large paw and gently drew the kitten behind a pile of rocks to hide.

A loud scraping sound pierced the cave. Flame's heart beat fast in his little chest as he listened to Ebony sharpening his claws on rock. A flash of anger glittered in the tiny kitten's emerald eyes. 'One day I will take back the throne my uncle stole from me!' he mewed bravely.

'And I do not doubt that you will

be a wise ruler, my prince,' Cirrus said, a smile creasing his wrinkled muzzle. He gave Flame's tiny head an affectionate lick.

A menacing shape almost filled the cave's entrance. Raising its powerful head, the enormous black lion shook its mane. Ebony growled again. Peering into the cave, he sniffed the air. 'Who's there? Show yourselves!' he roared.

'Go, Flame!' Cirrus urged through worn teeth. 'Go quickly! Use your kitten disguise and hide in the other world. Return again when you have grown strong and powerful!'

Silver sparks glittered in Flame's blue-grey fur. The tiny kitten mewed as he felt the power building inside him. He felt himself falling. Falling . . .

Chapter
* ONE *

'I'm here! I'm actually at Yew Lodge!'
Olivia Goddard whispered excitedly to
herself, as she entered the changing
rooms.

Everywhere she looked, there were
unfamiliar girls in grey skirts, white
blouses and blue cardigans. Olivia found
a space and started taking her things
out of her bag. She had just changed

into her new pink leotard when a group of girls walked in, giggling and whispering to each other. They looked about ten years old, the same as Olivia.

A small girl with silver-blonde hair and blue eyes stood nearest to Olivia.

Olivia smiled. 'Hi, I'm new here. I think I'm in your class,' she said.

'So what?' the blonde girl said rudely. She looked up at Olivia and smirked. 'What's the weather like up there?'

There were more muffled giggles and whispers from the other girls.

Olivia was used to being teased about her height. 'I don't know. My head's in the clouds,' she joked. 'What's it like down there?'

'That's told you, Lucy!' one of the

other girls said with a chuckle as Lucy
scowled and turned away.

The door banged as a girl with a
mop of bright-red hair came dashing
into the changing room. She dumped
her bag on the bench next to Olivia.

'Phew! Just made it. The bus was late,' she puffed. She gave Olivia a big grin. 'Serves me right, for not boarding here like everyone else, I suppose! Hi, I'm Tamsin!'

'Hi, I'm Olivia,' Olivia said, smiling.

Tamsin was slim with pale skin and freckles. She smelt of fresh air and spearmint chewing gum.

'Welcome to Yew Lodge!' Tamsin dragged a creased leotard and a pair of crumpled white ankle socks out of her bag. 'Are you a day girl, like me?'

'No, I'm boarding,' Olivia replied. 'My mum's only just dropped me off. I haven't even had time to unpack properly, but I didn't want to miss my first class. It feels a bit weird to be starting mid-term.'

'I bet it does,' Tamsin agreed. 'Have you met any of the others yet?'

'Only Lucy, but she wasn't exactly friendly,' Olivia said quietly.

Tamsin rolled her eyes. 'What a surprise. Not!' she whispered back. 'Lucy Castor thinks she's Miss Perfect. Don't take any notice of her.'

Olivia laughed, pleased to find that not everyone was so unfriendly.

Unfortunately, Lucy chose that moment to flounce past on her way to the studio.

'Ooh, look, Mariko!' she said to the pretty girl with high cheekbones and almond eyes by her side. 'Beanpole and Frizz are friends.'

Olivia's heart sank as she noticed Tamsin's face flush before she twisted her mass of curly red hair into a bun.

'I think you've got amazing hair,' Olivia said, hoping that Lucy's spiteful comment hadn't frightened off the only girl to be friendly to her so far.

'Thanks, Olivia,' Tamsin said with a wry chuckle. 'I guess it is a bit of a frizz – I have to use tons of this gel stuff to stop bits of it springing out and hanging in my eyes.'

Olivia, relieved to see that Tamsin hadn't been too bothered by Lucy, groaned in sympathy. 'My hair does that too.'

Tamsin held out the tube of hair gel. 'Try some of this.'

'Thanks.' Olivia squeezed some out and smoothed it on to her thick brown hair. In no time at all, she had coiled it round and pinned it into a neat bun. She sat down to tie her shoe ribbons.

Tamsin was tying hers too. 'Don't forget to tuck in the ends. Miss Frances hates flapping ribbons. She calls them pig's ears!' she said. A few moments later she jumped up. 'That's me done. Ready?'

Olivia nodded.

As she followed Tamsin into the large light studio with its shiny wooden floor, Olivia felt her stomach clench with nerves. Three entire walls were mirrored and a double barre ran round them. In one corner, a woman was seated at a piano.

'Here's Miss Frances,' Tamsin whispered as the teacher came in.

Olivia stared at the tiny, straight-backed woman. Frances Edwards had been a principal dancer with a famous ballet company. There was a photo of her dancing in *Giselle* in Olivia's ballet book, which had been a present for her tenth birthday.

'Good morning, class. Let's begin,' said Miss Frances, giving a signal to the pianist. Olivia and Tamsin faced the barre and, along with everyone else, began doing pliés in time to the music.

Olivia felt herself relaxing as she concentrated on the familiar exercises. She had been doing these movements since she was four years old. She knew that even the greatest dancers did them too, every single day.

Miss Frances walked around, adjusting the placing of a dancer's arm or leg. When she reached Olivia, she frowned. She made a chopping motion in the air and the piano stopped abruptly. 'You! Come out here,' she said sharply.

Olivia swallowed as she walked into the centre of the studio.

'You're new, aren't you? What's your name?' Miss Frances asked.

'Olivia Goddard,' Olivia answered. 'It . . . it's my first day.'

'Then why didn't you come and introduce yourself?' The teacher's stern eyes raked Olivia's face. 'It's very bad manners to just slip into my class without a word.'

'Slip into class? Gallop like a giraffe more like!' Lucy Castor sniggered from where she was standing.

Olivia tried to pretend she hadn't heard. 'I'm sorry, Miss Frances. I . . . I just didn't think,' she stammered, her face scarlet.

'Very well. We'll say no more about it. Where did you take ballet lessons?' asked Miss Frances more gently.

Olivia told her and explained that she had been taking ballet lessons twice a week.

Miss Frances nodded slowly. 'Well, you're going to have two classes a day now. So be prepared to work hard. You'll find ballet school a great challenge.'

'I hope so, Miss Frances. That's why I've come here,' Olivia said spiritedly.

Miss Frances's sharp eyes flashed with approval. 'Very well. Go back to the barre. I want to see you dance.'

Olivia went to the barre and took up a basic position. It felt like everybody was watching her, especially Lucy and Mariko. Tamsin caught her eye and gave her a thumbs-up sign.

As Miss Frances gave her instructions,

Olivia took a deep breath and began. After a few minutes, she felt the love of dancing sweep through her and she forgot to be self-conscious. By the time Miss Frances told her to stop, she was hot and sweaty and her muscles were tingling.

'You have style, but your technique could be improved,' Miss Frances said seriously. 'Take a rest now. Fetch a towel to wipe your face.'

'Yes, Miss Frances,' Olivia said numbly, as she went back into the changing room. She had tried her hardest, but it seemed she had a long way to go before she impressed Miss Frances.

Olivia went through to some wash basins and splashed her face with cold

water as she thought about what a
difficult morning it had been all round.
Yew Lodge seemed rather different to
the exciting place she had always
dreamed about.

Olivia sighed, drying her face on a
towel. Suddenly a bright silver flash
from out of the corner of her eye
stopped her in her tracks.

Olivia whirled round. 'Oh,' she
gasped, blinking hard.

At the far end of the shower room
crouched a tiny, fluffy, blue-grey kitten
with a round face and the most
enormous emerald-green eyes Olivia
had ever seen. Its fur and whiskers
seemed to glitter with thousands of tiny
stars.

Olivia rubbed her face with the
towel again — she'd obviously danced
too hard and was seeing things now!
She looked up from the towel. The
sparkles had gone, but the kitten was
still there. Perhaps it belonged to the
lodge.

She bent down. 'Hello, aren't you
gorgeous? Don't be scared. I won't
hurt you,' she crooned gently, reaching

out her hand. 'What's your name, then?'

'My name is Prince Flame,' the kitten mewed. 'Can you help me, please?'

Chapter
* TWO *

Olivia almost toppled over. She jerked
her hand back and stared at the kitten
in complete shock.

'Did . . . did you really just speak?'
she gasped, looking round wildly to see
if anyone was hiding nearby. She
wouldn't put it past Lucy to play a
trick on her.

The fluffy kitten was trembling all

over, but it sat up straight and pricked up its ears. Despite its tiny size it didn't seem to be afraid of her. 'Yes, I did. I am Flame, heir to the Lion Throne. Who are you?'

'I'm . . . um, Olivia Goddard,' Olivia stammered, her curiosity beginning to get the better of her shock. 'Where have you come from?'

'I am in disguise,' Flame mewed softly. 'I come from another world, far from here.'

'What? Like from outer space? But if . . . if you're disguised as a kitten, what are you re –' Olivia began and then stopped as a scary thought occurred to her. Maybe Flame was really an alien, with warty skin and millions of octopus arms! 'Wait! Maybe I don't want to know . . . !' she gabbled.

But it was too late. There was another flash, so bright this time that for a moment Olivia couldn't see a thing. She rubbed her eyes. When she looked again, she saw that where the tiny kitten had crouched there now stood a regal young lion with glittering white fur.

Olivia backed away in amazement.
'Flame?'

The lion looked at Olivia with its
emerald eyes and nodded slowly. But
before she could say anything else, he
vanished in a shower of sparkles and
appeared once more as a tiny, fluffy,
blue-grey kitten.

'Wow! You really are a lion prince!'
Olivia gasped, relieved and impressed at
the same time. 'But why would you
need my help?'

Flame gave a small shaky miaow. 'My Uncle Ebony. He is very powerful and has stolen my throne. He rules in my place and sends his spies to search for me and kill me.'

'Kill you?' Olivia asked, horrified.

'Yes. I must hide. Will you help me, Olivia?'

Olivia's heart went out to the tiny kitten – she knew exactly what it was like to feel all alone. 'I'd love to help you, Flame, but pets aren't allowed in ballet school,' she said, biting her lip. 'I don't even have my own room. There're eight of us in the dormitory. It would be impossible to hide you.'

Flame tilted his little round head. 'Not if I made myself invisible. Then no one will see me, except you.'

'Really? Well – if you can do that . . .'
Olivia came to a decision. She picked
Flame up gently and stroked his silky
ears. 'Right. You're living with me. I
won't let anybody hurt you! The only
thing is, I have to go back out soon.
My teacher will be wondering where I
am, so you'll have to become invisible
straight away. Is that OK?'

Flame didn't reply, but his whiskers crackled with electricity and his fluffy blue-grey fur glittered all over with silver sparkles that fizzed against Olivia's hands. She felt a warm tingling sensation down her back. It felt very strange, but not unpleasant.

'It is done. Only you can see me now,' Flame purred happily, as the sparks slowly faded away. 'Thank you, Olivia.'

'You're welcome.' Olivia smiled. 'I wonder what Tamsin will say, when I tell her about you.'

Flame stiffened. He stretched up one tiny blue-grey paw and touched her face.

'No! You must not tell anyone about me.'

'Really? I'm sure Tamsin's not like the other girls I've met here. She seems really nice.'

'I am sorry.' Flame looked up at her, his big green eyes serious. 'You cannot tell anyone about me. Promise, Olivia.'

Olivia thought about it. She felt a bit bad for keeping something so amazing from the friendly girl she had met that morning. But if it was the only way that Flame could stay with her, she knew what she must do.

'All right. I promise,' Olivia said. 'You'll be my secret. My secret magic kitten!'

Chapter
THREE

As Olivia went back to the studio, Flame padded along beside her. He spotted the piano and scampered straight over and curled up beneath it. Although Flame was invisible, Olivia couldn't help thinking that someone would notice the tiny blue-grey kitten. But, after a while, when no one did, she gradually relaxed.

Olivia saw that Miss Frances was coaching Tamsin. 'Concentrate! Keep your legs tight and don't sway backwards, Tamsin. Think of an imaginary line from the top of your head to your toe.'

Olivia stood and watched as Tamsin lifted one arm and leg in the melting, flowing movements of *battement fondu*. She was impressed. Tamsin was poised and elegant and could lift her pointed toe above the second barre.

'What are you staring at? Didn't they do real dancing where you come from, Beanpole?' Lucy hissed in Olivia's ear.

Mariko sniggered. 'They probably still wear clogs!'

Feeling much braver, now that she had Flame for a friend, Olivia gave the mean girls a fierce look. 'I've never worn clogs. But I wish I was wearing them right now!'

Mariko and Lucy moved away warily.

Miss Frances finished coaching Tamsin. 'Everyone choose partners,' she said. 'You'll work together for the rest of the class. Olivia, you will work with Tamsin.'

Olivia glanced over at Flame. He was watching her every move with alert green eyes. She couldn't help wondering what Miss Frances would say if she knew that there was a magic kitten in her class!

At 11 a.m. when class finished, all the pupils faced Miss Frances and bowed in a graceful *révérence*.

There was a buzz of noise as everyone filed out. 'Are you coming?' Tamsin called to Olivia.

'In a minute,' Olivia said, pretending to fiddle with her shoe ribbon. When everyone had gone, she went and picked Flame up. 'Did you enjoy watching your first ballet class?' she asked him.

His forehead wrinkled in a puzzled

frown. 'It was interesting, but I found those movements very strange. Are you training to be a warrior, Olivia?' he purred.

Olivia laughed. 'No! I want to be a ballerina.'

Flame blinked. 'What is a ball-er-ina?'

'A very special kind of dancer. You get to wear amazing costumes and dance on stage in front of lots of people,' Olivia explained simply. 'I've got a brilliant book with loads of photos of dancers. I'll show you sometime.'

'I would like that,' Flame mewed.

In the changing room, Flame sat licking his paws under the bench, invisible to all the other girls in Olivia's class.

'We have normal lessons now, until
the afternoon dance class,' Tamsin told
Olivia, doing up her grey skirt. 'I'll see
you in the classroom? I just have to
pop to the loo.'

'OK,' Olivia called after her. She
crouched down to the bench and

lowered her voice to a whisper. 'It
might be best if you get into my
school bag, Flame. It could look weird
if I seem to be carrying something that
no one can see!'

'That is a good idea.' Flame jumped
into the open bag.

'I suppose you're feeling pretty
pleased with yourself?' a familiar voice
behind her said.

Olivia didn't bother to look up. She
carried on making Flame comfortable
among the books and ballet kit. 'What
are you talking about, Lucy?'

'Don't act dumb! I saw you hanging
around in the studio, so you could suck
up to Miss Frances!' Lucy cried.

'That's rubbish! I was waiting for . . .
for . . .' Olivia tailed off, realizing that

she had been about to mention Flame.

Lucy's eyes flashed with temper. 'See! You can't deny it! You're just trying to be a rotten teacher's pet!' Her arm shot out and she grabbed Olivia's school bag.

'Hey! Give that back!' Olivia shouted.

But Lucy had already darted away. She drew back her arm and hurled the bag across the changing room.

'No!' Olivia gave a horrified gasp as her bag, with Flame inside, flew high into the air.

She ran forward in a desperate attempt to catch the soaring bag, but then stopped suddenly as a familiar warm tingling sensation ran up her spine.

Something strange was about to

happen – and Flame was definitely involved!

Olivia watched in amazement as the school bag seemed to slow down. It came to a dead halt, floating in mid-air for a heartbeat, before whizzing back towards Lucy. Smack! It hit her in the chest.

'Oof!' Lucy lost her balance and sat down hard on a bench. The girls' coats fell off their pegs and all landed on Lucy in a big messy pile.

'Aargh! Someone get them off me!' Lucy called, kicking her feet from underneath them.

Olivia quickly grabbed her bag before Lucy could get free, and hurried into the corridor. 'Flame! Are you all right?' she said, opening the zip wide.

Flame's bright-green eyes gleamed at her from the depths of the bag. 'I am fine,' he purred.

'Thank goodness!' Olivia breathed. She chuckled to herself as she headed for the classroom. 'That was brilliant, Flame! You should have seen Lucy's face when my bag zonked her!'

A howl of rage rang out as Lucy and Mariko burst into the corridor behind Olivia and Flame. 'I don't know what just happened. But I'm going to get that teacher's pet. Just you wait!' Lucy stormed.

Chapter
* FOUR *

Over the next week or so, Olivia
gradually settled into the school's
routine. At first, she found two dance
classes a day a real challenge. But the
exercises designed to strengthen her
feet and ankles, which Miss Frances set
her, helped a lot.

Olivia sat near Tamsin during normal
school lessons and at lunchtimes. Miss

Frances often chose them to partner each other. As the tallest girls in the class, they danced together well. Olivia was starting to enjoy herself much more now that she and Tamsin were becoming firm friends.

But as Tamsin wasn't boarding at Yew Lodge she went home before dinner every night. Olivia would have missed her a lot more if she hadn't had Flame. She wished like mad that she could tell Tamsin about the magic kitten, but a promise was a promise.

A spell of wet weather kept Olivia and Flame indoors in the evenings. As she didn't fancy watching TV or playing computer games, Olivia began going to the studio for another practice session. With Flame beside her, she worked harder at her dancing than she had ever done before.

'I will help you, Olivia,' Flame said one evening, raising a tiny paw.

A cloud of sparks shot towards Olivia, who was working on her leg extensions. Suddenly her outstretched leg shot straight up in front of her and almost banged into her nose.

'Flame!' she said reprovingly, trying not to giggle. 'Stop that! I have to do this by myself!'

'I am sorry,' Flame purred, looking crestfallen. 'I did not mean to interfere.'

'That's OK. I know you meant well,' she said, picking him up and giving him a cuddle. 'Come on. I've finished for tonight anyway.'

On her way up to the dorm, she passed Lucy and Mariko who ignored her as they usually did now – which was fine with Olivia.

'I think you really taught Lucy a lesson,' she said to Flame later, as he curled up beside her on the duvet.

Flame blinked at her. 'Perhaps, but I would not be too certain of that,' he purred sleepily.

★

At the end of class the following day,
Tamsin joined Olivia as they filed out
of the studio. 'Miss Frances is really
pleased with you,' she told her.

Olivia blinked at her. 'How can you
tell? She hardly says anything to me.'

Tamsin grinned. 'I know the signs,'
she said. 'She watches you when you're
not looking and I even caught her
smiling once!'

'Really?' Olivia felt a glow of pride.
Maybe all her extra hard work was
starting to have an effect. She looked
down at her feet where Flame was
padding alongside her, invisible to
everyone else, and smiled as she
thought about how much fun she was
having at ballet school now.

Miss Frances raised her voice. 'Olivia!

After you get changed, I want you to come to the shoe department with me.'

Olivia's heart beat fast. This could only mean one thing. She was going to get her very first pair of pointe shoes!

'I knew it! Congratulations!' Tamsin said, giving her a hug back in the changing rooms. 'I got my pointe shoes last year. I remember feeling like a real dancer for the first time!'

Olivia waited until everyone had gone and then lifted Flame into her school bag. 'Let's go and find Miss Frances. This is so exciting!' she whispered to him.

Flame was fascinated by the shoe department. He jumped up on to the counters and sniffed at the rows of shoes, which were being dyed to match some brightly coloured costumes.

Miss Frances supervised while Olivia's feet were measured. Then came the wonderful moment when a cardboard shoebox was lifted down from a shelf. Olivia's heart beat fast as she held the box in her hand. She opened it slowly and took out the beautiful pale-peach satin shoes, with their printed gold labels and blunt tips.

'You have done very well. It's a special time for a young dancer, when she gets her first pair of pointe shoes. Enjoy this moment, Olivia,' Miss Frances said, smiling.

'Thank you. I will,' Olivia said, her eyes pricking with tears of pride and happiness.

After checking them for the correct
fit, Olivia was allowed to take her new
shoes away. She sat on her bed in the
dorm to sew ribbons into them. Flame
sat nearby on the window sill, watching
her with pricked ears.

Olivia finished sewing and held up a
shoe. 'Isn't it the most gorgeous thing
you've ever seen?' she said admiringly.

Flame leapt on to the bed. He tapped
the hard satin-covered tips with a tiny

paw, his bright emerald eyes looking puzzled. 'Why do they make you strap these on to your feet? Is it a punishment?'

Olivia laughed and lifted him into her lap. 'No! They let us dance on the very tips of our toes, *en pointe*, and make us look light and delicate.'

'Humans do some very odd things!' Flame lifted a blue-grey paw and flexed his sharp little claws. 'I would never cover my paws!'

'I think that's very sensible!' Olivia said, grinning to herself as a cute picture of Flame wearing tiny ballet shoes filled her head!

The following day, when she wore her new shoes in class and began simple exercises at the barre, Olivia felt very grown up. It would be a long time before she could dance *en pointe* for any length of time, but this was definitely a major step towards her dream of becoming a ballerina!

Chapter
* FIVE *

'See you tomorrow, Tamsin!' Olivia
waved goodbye to her friend at the
school gate and then turned back into
the school grounds.

Olivia had brought her ballet book
outside with her. It was a gorgeous
warm evening and she planned to find
a quiet place to sit and read it with
Flame. She wandered down a

flower-bordered path, with him scampering along, whiskers twitching as he sniffed the interesting scents. Every now and then he pounced on a twig or chased a feather. Suddenly, he gave an eager mew and leapt into the air to chase a bumblebee.

'Watch out it doesn't sting you!' Olivia warned as Flame dived head first into the middle of a patch of yellow pansies, leaving only his fluffy little back legs and short tail on view. A moment later he reappeared, his nose dusted with sticky yellow pollen. 'What *do* you look like?' she said, chuckling.

The sunset cast a soft glow on to a long, sloping lawn, with an old stone well in the centre. After the recent rain,

water had gathered in muddy puddles
at the bottom of the slope.

'Perfect!' Olivia sighed happily, as she
settled beside a flower bed on the dry
grass at the top.

Flame jumped into her lap and
curled up, purring contentedly.

Olivia opened her book and began
turning the thick glossy pages. She
knew all the photos off by heart, but it
was fun showing them to Flame. 'This
is Darcey Bussell, one of my favourite
ballerinas. She's tall, like me,' she told
him. 'Here she is as Princess Aurora in
The Sleeping Beauty. And this is Sylvie
Guillem; she's amazing . . .'

Olivia was so engrossed in her book
that she didn't notice Lucy and Mariko
coming along the path towards her.

'All by yourself, now that Tamsin's
gone home?' Lucy called.

'Aw, diddums! She hasn't got any
friends,' said Mariko.

Olivia looked up. 'If it's a choice of
having no friends or having you two,
it's no contest!' she murmured.

Lucy came over and stood looking
down at her. 'You think you're so
clever, don't you?'

Olivia raised an eyebrow. 'Do I get a prize if I get the answer right?'

Lucy's blue eyes narrowed with anger. She leaned down and grabbed the ballet book.

Flame was flicked sideways. He leapt into the air and landed in the middle of a nearby flower bed on all fours. Olivia glanced at Flame to check that he was all right before springing to her feet and facing Lucy.

'Give me my book back, or else!' she demanded.

'Why don't you try and make me?' Lucy taunted, skipping backwards. She pretended to drop the book and then caught it by one cover, so that the pages flapped.

'Don't you dare tear it!' Olivia

warned. 'That book was a present and it cost a lot of money!'

Mariko glanced uncertainly at Lucy. 'It does look really expensive. Maybe you should give it back.'

'Don't be soft!' Lucy's face lit up with an idea. 'Come on!' she called to Mariko, already running down the slope.

The puddles! Olivia groaned,
knowing what was coming.

Lucy raised the book high above her
head.

Olivia felt a warm tingling down her
spine once again. Time seemed to stand
still. From where Flame was hidden in
the flower bed, she saw a glowing,
sparkly cloud rise. A tiny paw appeared
and a shimmering blue lightning bolt
streaked through the air.

The tiny blue bolt struck the book,
just as Lucy went to fling it into the
puddle. The book didn't move. It stuck
firmly to Lucy's hand.

'Ooh!' Lucy gasped, almost tottering
forward off balance. She shook her
hand, trying desperately to let go
of it.

'Mariko, help! I can't let go of it!' she
gasped.

Mariko reached out and grabbed the
other end. She tugged and pulled, but
couldn't get it out of Lucy's grip.
Shaking her head, she stepped

backwards and dragged Lucy and the book with her.

'Hey! Stop pulling me about!' complained Lucy.

'I can't help it! Now I can't let go of it either!' Mariko wailed.

The two of them lumbered about crab-like, pushing and pulling as they tried to get their hands unstuck.

Olivia bit back a grin as she sidled over to the flower bed. 'How long will they be stuck like that?' she whispered to Flame.

His whiskery little face peered out at her. 'Only until you touch the book.'

Tempting as it was to leave them there, Olivia strolled over to Lucy and Mariko and reached for her book. 'I think that's mine!'

First Mariko and then Lucy pinged backwards, just as if they'd bounced off a trampoline. There were two enormous splashes as they both landed flat on their faces in the puddle.

Lucy sat up covered in mud, her silver-blonde hair drooping like a big cowpat over one eye. 'What . . . what just happened?' she burbled.

Mariko staggered out of the puddle, dripping mud. 'Just look at the state of me! If you hadn't grabbed that book, this wouldn't have happened!' she grumbled.

'Oh, stop whining and help me up!' Lucy shouted.

'Get up by yourself!' Mariko shouted back.

Olivia left them arguing with each other. As she walked back up the lawn,

chuckling to herself, Flame jumped out
of the flower bed and trotted after her,
leaving a few telltale blue sparkles
crackling behind him.

Chapter
* SIX *

'I have good news, everyone,' Miss
Frances announced in class a few days
later. 'You're going to be doing the
Garland Dance from Act 1 of *The
Sleeping Beauty* for the school
performance at the end of term.'

Olivia and Tamsin exchanged excited
looks.

'*The Sleeping Beauty*'s one of my

favourite ballets,' Olivia said dreamily.

'Mine too,' Tamsin agreed excitedly. 'I wonder what our costumes will be like.'

No one could talk about anything else. The excited buzz of conversation became even louder when Miss Frances showed the girls some samples of pastel-coloured fabric and delicate flower trims.

'You may choose the colour of your costumes. You'll be wearing classic tutus and matching headdresses, made by the wardrobe department,' she said with a rare smile.

Everyone gathered round eagerly. Olivia chose a pale-oyster silk, trimmed with tiny pink rosebuds. Tamsin chose pale grey, trimmed with blue forget-me-nots.

'Isn't this brilliant?' Tamsin said. 'We're having our costumes made, just like dancers in the ballet company!'

While Tamsin and the others were totally engrossed in deciding on their costumes Olivia sidled across the studio and stood by the piano, where Flame was stretched out in a patch of warm sun.

'Mum and Dad are going to be so proud when they see me in my first ballet-school production! I can't wait to phone them tonight and tell them all about it!' she whispered to him. 'Are you looking forward to it too?'

Flame had been dozing. He lifted his little head and nodded sleepily. 'I hope very much that I will be here to see you dance.'

'Be here? Of course you will. Where else would you be?' Olivia asked, confused.

'If my enemies . . .' Flame began.

'Girls! Get into position to learn the first steps, please.' Olivia missed the rest of Flame's reply as Miss Frances's voice carried across the studio.

'I'd better go, Flame. I'll come and

get you after class.' Olivia bit her lip worriedly as she took up position next to Tamsin. She knew in her heart of hearts that Flame would have to leave one day, but she couldn't bear to even think about it just yet!

Her worries faded gradually as she worked hard to learn the complicated steps for the Garland Dance. Tamsin seemed to get the hang of them quite quickly, but it took Olivia many tries before she got them right.

'Again!' Miss Frances ordered. 'The arms are held like this!' She made the pupils dance the sequence over and over again.

Every movement had to be perfect, the head held just so, the toe pointed at the right angle. Miss Frances was

very difficult to please. Usually Olivia
loved every second of dance class, but
today she was quite glad to have
normal school lessons.

As Olivia bent down at the end of
class to let Flame jump into her school
bag, she winced a bit.

Flame immediately pricked up his ears.
'Is something wrong?' he purred softly.

'It's just my feet. They're a bit sore,'
Olivia said.

Flame mewed with concern. 'Shall I make the hurt go away?'

Olivia smiled. She had decided not to ask Flame again about when he might leave – he seemed happy to be here with her. 'Thanks, Flame,' she whispered. 'But it's just my body getting used to hard work. As I get stronger it won't hurt as much. It's just part of being a dancer. Don't worry about me. I love it here. I feel like the luckiest girl in the world and I wouldn't change a single thing. And that includes having you here!'

After another week of rehearsing to the piano, Miss Frances put on a CD of the beautiful music for the Garland Dance. Olivia was surprised how

different it felt to dance to an
orchestra. Now the work of getting
the dance perfect started all over
again.

The girls had begun to do class
wearing practice tutus, to get used to
dancing in costume. One morning, at
the end of the class, Olivia was slipping
hers off, when Miss Frances called
everyone together.

'We shall perform the dance in two
rows,' Miss Frances told everyone. In
the back row will be . . .' She called
out a number of names, including Lucy
and Mariko. 'And in the front row will
be Olivia, Tamsin . . .'

Olivia hardly heard the rest of the
names. She couldn't believe it. She was
going to dance in the front row!

'Did you hear that, Tamsin? Isn't it brilliant?' she said to her friend, as she placed the practice tutu upside down on the special stand in the corner.

Tamsin was drinking from a bottle of water. She wiped her mouth and grinned. 'You've worked really hard. You deserve it,' she said generously.

'No one's going to be able to see me in the back row, with Beanpole clumping around in front of us!' Lucy complained loudly.

Miss Frances frowned as she turned to Lucy. 'The dancers with the best technique will be in the front row. If you want to join them, my advice is to work a lot harder!' she snapped. 'Olivia has put in hours of extra practice. Perhaps you should too.'

Lucy's pretty face turned bright red.
She walked over to stand beside
Mariko.

'I can't stand that teacher's pet. I
hope she gets double chickenpox and
then I can have her place,' she
muttered.

Olivia was hurt but she pretended
not to hear. No matter what she did or
didn't do, Lucy and Mariko were never

going to like her. *It's just a fact of life, she thought, like having blisters and sore feet, and I've just got to get used to it.*

Chapter
SEVEN

'Only a few days now until the end of
term. I can't believe how quickly the
time's gone. I'm looking forward to
seeing you both. Bye, Mum. Give my
love to Dad.' Olivia replaced the phone
after speaking to her parents on Sunday
afternoon.

She turned to smile at Flame. 'Mum
and Dad love to hear all the news. I

told them that we've started rehearsing on stage and everything. They're really excited about coming to the school production. I just hope I don't mess up!'

'You will be fine. You are working so hard to be a good dancer,' Flame purred.

'Thanks, Flame!' Olivia said, stroking his soft little ears.

A group of girls from her class walked past. 'Hi, Olivia,' one of them called. 'We're going to watch a video of *The Nutcracker* in the common room. Do you want to come?'

Olivia loved the *Nutcracker* ballet, but she knew she really ought to take Flame outside. He'd spent a lot of time indoors while she had been doing extra practice in the studio. 'Thanks, but I think I'll catch up with you later, if that's OK. I'm going outside to get some fresh air,' she said to the girls.

'OK. See you,' they called as they walked off.

'Come on, Flame. I bet you'd love a run around outside.'

Flame nodded eagerly as he followed her out into the school grounds. Olivia strolled past the tennis courts. There was no one playing tennis today. Most pupils had gone home for the weekend to visit their parents, leaving only the boarders.

It was very quiet in the grounds. Olivia spotted some pink roses in the bed with the yellow pansies. As she stopped to smell one of them, Flame darted past in pursuit of a huge wood pigeon.

'You've got no chance of catching that,' she said, chuckling to herself as he scrambled under a bush after it. The pigeon was as big as he was!

Olivia wandered down the winding path to the sloping lawn with the old well in the centre. She sat and watched a squirrel loping across the grass, while she waited for Flame to come and find her.

After five minutes or so, when he hadn't appeared, she went to look for him. 'Flame?' she called softly, retracing her steps along the path, peering into flower beds and parting the bushes. 'Flame? Where are you?'

There was no answering miaow.

Olivia started to feel worried. Where could he be? What if Flame's enemies had found him already? They might have hurt him or worse!

Suddenly she heard a little wail of distress. It was coming from the direction of the lawn, behind her. With her heart racing, Olivia whipped round and dashed back there.

'Oh!' she gasped.

Lucy and Mariko stood in the centre
of the lawn. Lucy had both hands
tightly wrapped around Flame's middle.
His bottom half was dangling in mid-
air.

Flame must have been so engrossed
in playing with the wood pigeon that

he had forgotten to stay invisible! Now he couldn't do any magic without giving himself away.

'Stop wriggling!' Lucy said crossly, squeezing harder, as Flame gave another howl and lashed his tiny tail.

Olivia had had just about enough of Lucy and Mariko. Her chest tightened with anger. 'Put Fla . . . that kitten down! You're hurting him!' she shouted.

Lucy glared at Olivia. 'What are you stressing about, Beanpole? It's not your kitten!'

Yes, he is! Olivia wanted to shout, but even now she knew that she couldn't tell them that. 'Give him to me or else!' she demanded, rushing forward with clenched fists.

'Leg it!' Lucy shouted to Mariko,
zooming across the lawn.

Olivia shot after her, her long legs
eating up the grass.

Lucy glanced fearfully over her
shoulder and then stopped abruptly at
the well. She dangled Flame over the
widely spaced bars covering the
opening above the empty black space.

'Back off! Or I'll drop him in!' she shouted.

Olivia froze. 'You wouldn't!' she gasped.

Lucy's blue eyes glittered. 'Don't you come any nearer. Weird things happen when you're around!'

Flame's back legs pedalled the air. He screeched loudly with fear.

'Please don't hurt him!' Olivia begged. 'Look, I just want the kitten. I didn't mean to lose my temper with you,' she said reasonably.

'Give him to her, Lucy,' Mariko urged. 'Let her go and find out who it belongs to. Then we can go inside and watch the video.'

'Shut up! Both of you!' Lucy snapped.

Olivia gulped. Lucy had a hard, mean look on her face. She looked capable of anything. Her mind whirled. What could she do? 'I'll . . . I'll do a deal with you,' she blurted out. 'I'll give you my ballet book for the kitten!'

Lucy wavered. 'Really? Swear on this kitten's life that you'll let me keep the book.'

'OK. I swear,' Olivia said solemnly.

'You heard that, Mariko!' Lucy crowed. She looked back at Olivia. 'You have to keep your promise now or we'll tell everyone that you're a rotten liar and a cheat.'

Olivia didn't care. She felt weak with relief. 'Whatever. You can go and get the book yourself. It's in the cupboard next to my bed.'

Lucy backed slowly away from the well. 'Here!' She thrust Flame into Olivia's arms. 'I was only kidding, anyway! I hope it takes you hours to find its owner. Come on, Mariko. I'm going to the dormitory to get *my* book!' She ran off, followed by Mariko.

Olivia held Flame's little trembling body to her chest. His tiny heart was beating fast against her hands. 'It's OK, Flame. You're safe now,' she crooned softly.

'Thank you for saving me, Olivia.' Flame gave an especially loud purr and reached up a tiny paw to pat her cheek. 'I am very sorry that you have lost your book.'

'It doesn't matter. You're more important to me than any old book. I

nearly died on the spot when I
thought Lucy was going to drop you
into that well!' Olivia said.

She realized that she would do
anything to protect Flame.

Chapter
EIGHT

'We're collecting our costumes for the dress rehearsal on stage this morning!' Olivia swept Flame into her arms and shot down the stairs to the wardrobe department. 'Can you believe that the performance is only the day after tomorrow?'

Flame shook his head. 'I have been here with you for a few weeks now.

The time has gone by very fast.'

'I reckon your uncle's spies have given up looking for you. Maybe you can stay here with me forever,' Olivia said.

Flame looked up at her with gentle green eyes. 'That is not possible, Olivia. My destiny is in my own world.'

'I know,' Olivia said sadly. She didn't even want to think about Flame leaving.

Tamsin was already in the wardrobe department when Olivia and Flame arrived. 'It's amazing in here, isn't it?' Tamsin said, pointing to the huge rolls of satins, chiffons and velvets in every colour imaginable.

Olivia quickly put Flame down on a bench, before Tamsin noticed that she seemed to be holding something that she couldn't see! He scampered past a woman sitting at a sewing machine and then settled down to watch another woman, hand-sewing sequins on to a sky-blue tutu.

Olivia caught her breath when she saw her costume. It had a pale-orchid silk bodice, with thin straps trimmed with tiny pink rosebuds. The stiff skirt was held out by many layers of cream net. Her headdress was a band of matching pink rosebuds and crystal beads.

'Oh! It's even more beautiful than I expected,' she sighed, holding it up against her.

Tamsin was cradling her pale-grey costume in her arms. 'Mine's gorgeous too. I can't wait for dress rehearsal!'

The rest of the class collected their costumes and then everyone trooped along to the school's theatre, where Miss Frances was waiting.

'Wow! Look at this!' Olivia said, peering around the stage.

Everything was almost ready for the

main performance. There was a dark-
blue backcloth, with tiny lights for
stars. The colourful scenery had been
painted to look like the inside of a
fairy-tale castle.

The dress rehearsal was exciting, but
very hard work, as Miss Frances was
even more strict than usual. Olivia
concentrated fully on getting every step
right. If she even started thinking about
dancing in front of a full audience, her
tummy did a sickening backflip.

When the rehearsal was over, Miss
Frances gave a small smile. 'That went
quite well. Off you all go and get
changed. I'll see you this afternoon.'

Olivia was practising her pointe work
at the barre as afternoon class began.

Tamsin joined her, beginning some warm-up stretches. 'I just saw Lucy reading your ballet book in the common room. When I asked her about it, she said you gave it to her,' she said, frowning.

Olivia nodded, feeling awful that she couldn't let Tamsin know why. 'Yes, I did.'

'How come? You can't stand her any more than I can!' Tamsin's eyes narrowed suspiciously. When Olivia looked away, she held up her hands. 'OK, you don't have to tell me anything. But I'll help you get your book back if you like.'

'Thanks, Tamsin, but it doesn't matter now,' Olivia said. She glanced across at the tiny ball of blue-grey fur on top of the piano. She still had what really mattered to her – Flame!

Miss Frances clapped her hands for attention. 'Places, everyone. Let's go through the Garland Dance again. I want you all perfect for tomorrow.'

As Olivia waited for the music to begin, the door of the studio opened. A frail-looking elderly woman, with black hair and a silver walking stick, came in.

Miss Frances quickly fetched a chair for her.

'It's Nina Svetlova!' Tamsin whispered. 'She founded this school!'

'She must be going to take class!' Olivia guessed, glancing at the almost legendary ex-prima ballerina.

Nina banged on the floor with her stick. 'Begin!' she ordered. She watched everyone closely, making corrections when she thought they were needed. 'No, no! It's not meant to be like that!' she said, pointing her stick at Lucy. 'You are too stiff. Move your arms like this. Hold up your head and smile!'

Lucy pressed her mouth together as

she danced. Her face was beetroot red.

Then Nina turned her attention to Olivia. Olivia danced for all she was worth, trying not to think about the sharp critical eyes watching her.

'Good!' said Nina, when Olivia finished. 'That is how the dance should be! You!' she said, pointing to Lucy. 'Watch and learn!'

There were hushed whispers as the class ended and everyone went to get changed. Mariko had her arm around Lucy, who was in tears.

'Phew! I thought Miss Frances was strict, but she's got nothing on Miss Svetlova,' Olivia said to Tamsin. 'She must have made us do the Garland Dance about a hundred times! And she had a real go at Lucy! I couldn't help feeling sorry for her.'

Tamsin shrugged. 'It's her own fault. She should make more effort.' She flashed Olivia a pleased grin. 'But I think we both did OK!'

Olivia nodded, feeling a flush of pride. She was going to phone her parents as soon as she could and tell them that the famous Nina Svetlova had just coached her!

Chapter
* NINE *

Olivia woke the following morning with butterflies in her tummy. 'This is the day! Mum and Dad will be on their way here soon,' she said to Flame. 'It's the final dress rehearsal this morning.'

She jumped out of bed and got dressed quickly. Usually Flame followed her everywhere, but today he seemed reluctant to get off the bed.

'Hey! Sleepyhead,' she teased gently.
'Are you coming?'

Flame peeped out of his cosy nest in
the duvet, with dull, troubled eyes. 'I
think I will stay here for a bit longer,'
he mewed quietly.

'What's wrong? Don't you feel well?'
Olivia said, beginning to feel alarmed.

'I think my enemies are getting
close,' Flame told her with a tiny
shudder. 'If I stay very still, they may
pass by.'

'Oh, no!' Olivia gasped. She was dreading the moment when Flame would have to leave, but it was a million times worse to think of him being hurt. 'That's it. I'm going to stay here with you. I'll say I have a tummy ache or something . . .'

'No. It would draw attention to me. You cannot miss this important rehearsal,' Flame mewed.

Olivia knew Flame was right, but she felt torn. 'All right, I'll go. But I'll come back and check on you when I can. You *will* still be here when I get back, won't you?' She was distraught at the thought of not being able to say goodbye.

Flame curled up and tucked his tail round his tiny body. He gave a muffled little mew. 'I hope so.'

Olivia's heart was heavy as she went to the dance studio.

'Are you OK?' asked Tamsin, as soon as she caught sight of Olivia's pale face.

'Yes, I'm fine,' Olivia said, pulling herself together with a huge effort.

She managed to push her worries about Flame to the back of her mind and somehow concentrated fully on her dancing, but the moment rehearsal finished Olivia dashed straight back up to the dorm.

Flame was on the landing, ears pricked and his little tail sticking straight up perkily. The fearful look had faded from his emerald eyes. He mewed a greeting as Olivia bounded up the stairs two at a time towards him.

'Flame!' Olivia cried happily. 'I was so scared that you'd be gone!'

'I sensed my enemies pass. They may still return, but for now I am safe,' Flame purred.

'Oh, I'm so glad!' Olivia bent down to stroke his soft fur. 'Come on. It's almost lunchtime. I'll see if I can smuggle something extra delicious out for you!'

With a joyful little miaow, Flame jumped into her arms.

Olivia sat in the common room with Tamsin. Flame was curled up invisibly by her side. Normal lessons had finished early and the entire school seemed to be in upheaval as final preparations for the performance were made.

Olivia felt so nervous that she couldn't keep still. She kept jumping up and pacing about. Flame seemed to have been infected by her nerves. One minute he was sitting down, the next he was pacing behind her.

'What time is it?' Olivia asked Tamsin.

Tamsin grinned. 'Five minutes later than when you just asked me!'

'Sorry,' Olivia said. 'I hate waiting about. If only there was something to do.'

'We're supposed to be relaxing,' Tamsin said. 'There's still over an hour before we need to start getting our make-up and costumes on.'

'It's no good. I feel like I've got jumping beans in my tummy! I think I'll go and see if Mum and Dad have arrived.'

'Good idea,' Tamsin said. 'You must be dying to see them after all these weeks. Not like me; I have to see my parents every day. I'll stay here and read my magazine. I'll see you in Wardrobe later.'

'OK,' Olivia sang out as she hurried
out of the common room. She couldn't
understand how Tamsin could be so
calm when she was exactly the
opposite!

With Flame in her shoulder bag,
Olivia went outside to check the car
park, but there was no sign of her
parents' car yet.

'Never mind. They'll be here soon,'
she said to Flame. 'Let's go back inside.'

Flame answered with a sleepy purr
from the depths of the bag.

Olivia put her hand inside, and
stroked Flame gently. She wandered
down the corridor and found herself
heading down towards the wardrobe
room. Maybe she'd go and have
another look at her costume.

Just before she got to Wardrobe, she
saw that the door to a normally empty
room stood wide open. It was crammed
with dress rails full of glittering
costumes.

'Oh, look!' Olivia said delightedly,
spotting her costume on the end of the
rail nearest to her.

But as she reached for the hanger,
Olivia caught a movement from the
corner of her eye. A large dark shadow

was climbing the wall of the corridor. Something was coming towards them.

'He is close. I can sense him,' growled a harsh, cruel voice.

Olivia froze. Flame's enemies. They were here!

Chapter
* TEN *

Olivia didn't hesitate. She turned on her heel and ran. There was a cloakroom just past Wardrobe. As soon as she reached it, she hurtled inside.

'Flame! You must go! Now!' she hissed, opening her bag. 'I've just seen your uncle's spies. They're right behind us!

Flame gave a startled mew and

jumped out of her bag. His fur all
stood on end and his ears were
flattened. A flash of bright white light
filled the whole cloakroom and Olivia
felt a shower of sparks come down all
around her.

She blinked, half blinded. When she
looked again, Flame had gone.

Olivia stood there, stunned. She
couldn't believe what had just
happened. Flame had left her without
even saying goodbye!

She went back into the corridor in a
daze and walked slowly back towards
the room with the rails of costumes.

Lucy and Mariko were there now,
collecting their costumes. Olivia
frowned. She seemed to remember that
Lucy's costume was pale violet, so why

was she holding up a pale-orchid tutu? As Olivia drew nearer, Mariko spotted her. She gave a start and nudged Lucy, who whipped round with a guilty expression on her face.

It was a moment before Olivia noticed the scissors in Lucy's hand. And then she saw the two big cuts on the bodice of her beautiful tutu.

Olivia gasped in disbelief at her ruined costume. There was a tight feeling in her chest, but instead of feeling angry, she just felt sad and weary. Flame had gone and she still couldn't really take that in. Hot tears began spilling down her face.

Mariko's face crumpled too. 'I'm really sorry,' she murmured.

Lucy dropped the costume and the

scissors. 'I was only going to cut the
rosebuds off. The scissors slipped . . .'
she said in a shaky voice. 'You . . . you
won't tell Miss Frances, will you? I'll
get expelled.'

'Just clear off and leave me alone!'
Olivia sobbed.

Lucy's lips trembled. She turned and
ran off as fast as she could. Mariko
hesitated, looking at Olivia like she
wanted to say something, but then
turned and hurried after Lucy.

Olivia picked up her ruined costume.
There was no time to repair it, even if
it were possible to mend the damage.
She couldn't dance in the performance
now.

Suddenly her spine began to tingle.
She heard a crackle of sparks and
slowly turned round.

'Flame!' Olivia cried, as his tiny blue-
grey form crawled out from under the
dress rail. 'You're still here! How? What?'

Flame's emerald eyes glittered. 'I have
laid a false scent trail. But my enemies
are still close. I cannot stay for long.'

She threw herself to her knees and picked him up. She thought her heart might burst with happiness. 'Oh, I'm so glad you've come back!'

'I wanted to be here to see you dance,' he mewed solemnly, rubbing the top of his furry little head against her cheek.

'But how can . . .' Olivia began, looking down at the slashed bodice of her tutu.

Flame lifted his paw and a fine sprinkle of silver sparks shot out. They drifted on to the tutu like glittering talcum powder. The rips in the bodice edges drew together by themselves and the slashes faded slowly, until the only thing Olivia could see was the pale glint of the silky-smooth fabric.

She held up the tutu. 'It's as good as new,' she said delightedly. 'Oh, Flame. Thank you so much.'

'You are welcome. I think it is time for you to get ready now!' Flame mewed, showing his little sharp teeth in a grin.

Olivia stood on the stage next to Tamsin. Her mind was a blank. She felt sure that she had forgotten every step that Miss Frances had taught her.

Her heart beat fast as the first bars of the Garland Dance began. Slowly, the curtain was raised.

Olivia took a deep breath and began dancing.

Her feet seemed to move by themselves as she drifted lightly across the stage, in perfect time with the other dancers. In the bright light, the stage set was a glittering fairy realm. Olivia danced with her heart and soul, losing herself completely in the spirit of the dance. All too soon the music began to fade and she swept into a graceful bow.

The audience broke into enthusiastic applause.

Olivia quickly glanced at the delighted faces, trying to spot her parents. With so many rows of seats, she couldn't see them, but she was sure they were there somewhere.

The music changed and Olivia glided on a cloud of happiness into the wings with the other girls.

As soon as they were backstage, Tamsin ran over and gave her a hug. 'How amazing was that?' she cried.

'It was incredible! Like a dream,' Olivia said.

Miss Frances appeared from the shadows. 'Well done!' she said, giving them both a hug. 'I'm very proud of you both.'

Olivia and Tamsin were too shocked to speak. *Wonders would never cease,*

Olivia thought, biting back a grin, *Miss Frances seemed almost human.*

'I've some wonderful news. Nina Svetlova was very impressed when she saw you in class the other day. She's recommended that you both move up a class next term!' Miss Frances said.

'That's fantastic!' Tamsin said. She grabbed Olivia and they jumped up and down with their mouths open in silent squeals of excitement.

Lucy suddenly appeared with Mariko backstage. 'I still don't know how she repaired the costume so quickly . . .' Olivia heard her whispering.

But when she saw Olivia and Tamsin with Miss Frances, Lucy stopped. Her eyes flickered worriedly between Olivia and the teacher. 'What . . . what are you talking to Miss Frances about?' she asked sweetly.

Olivia knew that Lucy thought she was snitching.

'Not everything's about you, Lucy. You tell them our news, Tamsin!' Olivia called over her shoulder, already rushing off to find Flame.

She couldn't wait to tell him the brilliant news!

Olivia ran into the shadows of the prop room at the back of the stage, but before she could even speak, there was a blinding silver flash and a shower of sparks. A regal young white lion stood looking solemnly at Olivia. An older grey lion stood next to him.

Flame raised his big white paw in farewell and Olivia knew that his trick to escape his enemies had been discovered. This time, Flame was leaving for good.

'Be well, be strong and dance with a brave heart, Olivia,' Flame rumbled in a deep velvety voice. And then he and the older lion vanished.

'I'll never forget you, Flame,' Olivia whispered, her heart aching. But at least she had been able to see him one more time. She knew she would always remember her wonderful magic kitten.

'Olivia, love!' called a voice. 'We just got here in time to see the performance. You were marvellous!'

She looked up and saw her parents standing backstage, beaming with pride.

'Mum! Dad! I've got some fantastic news!' Olivia called, running towards them.

Win a Magic Kitten goody bag!

An urgent and secret message has been left for Flame
from his own world, where his evil uncle is
still hunting for him.

Two words from the message can be found in royal lion
crowns hidden in *A Glittering Gallop* and *Sparkling Steps*.
Find the hidden words and put them together to complete
the message. Send it in to us and each month we will
put every correct message in a draw and pick out one lucky
winner who will receive a purrfect Magic Kitten gift!

Send your secret message, name and address on a postcard to:
Magic Kitten Competition
Puffin Books
80 Strand
London WC2R 0RL

Hurry, Flame needs your help!

Good luck!

puffin.co.uk

Visit:
penguin.co.uk/static/cs/uk/0/competition/terms.html
for full terms and conditions

Magic Kitten

A Glittering Gallop

Flame needs to find a purrfect new friend!

And that's how Zoe's summer of horse riding gallops by when a lovable calico kitten turns up . . .

puffin.co.uk

Magic Kitten

Classroom Chaos
978–0–141–32015–1

Star Dreams
978–0–141–32016–8

A Summer Spell
978–0–141–32014–4

Double Trouble
978–0–141–32017–5

A Circus Wish
978–0–141–32154–7

Sparkling Steps
978–0–141–32155–4

Moonlight Mischief
978–0–141–32153–0

A Glittering Gallop
978–0–141–32156–1

Coming Soon . . .

Seaside Mystery
978–0–141–32198–1

Firelight Friends
978–0–141–32199–8

puffin.co.uk